Best **FRIENDS** Forever!

It's always an **ADVENTURE** when we're together!

All for one!
¡TODOS JUNTOS!

TIME FOR **Adventure!**

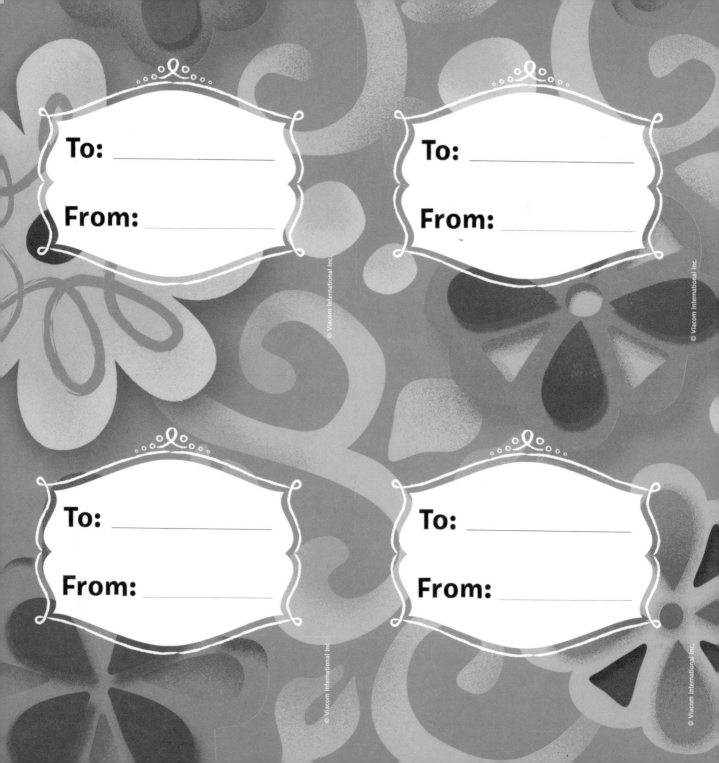

To: _____

From: _____

To: _____

From: _____

To: _____

From: _____

To: _____

From: _____

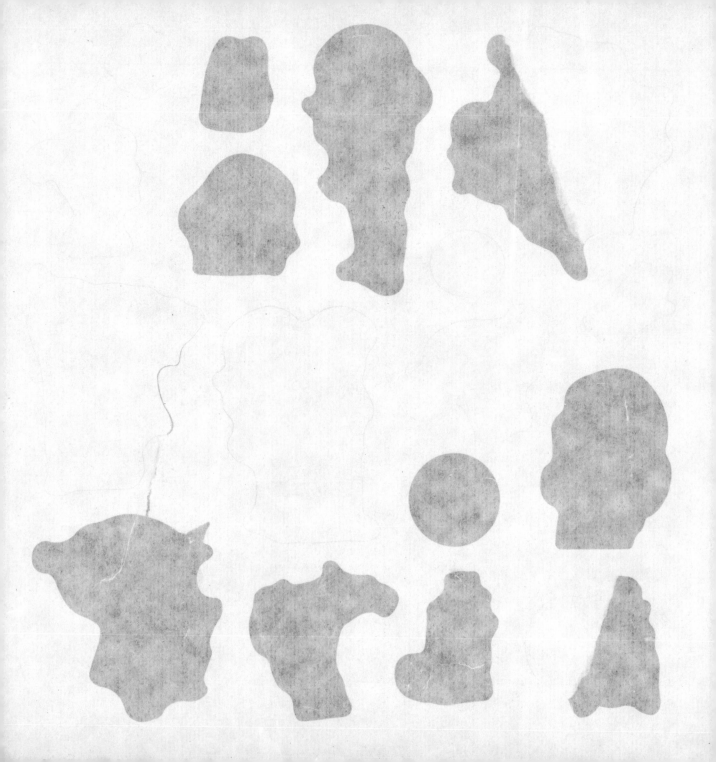

Boots and Dora Forever!

Adapted by Mary Tillworth
Based on the teleplay "Welcome Home" by Chris Gifford
Illustrated by Dave Aikins

A Random House PICTUREBACK® Book
Random House 🏠 New York

© 2016 Viacom International Inc. All rights reserved. Published in the United States by Random House Children's Books, a division of Penguin Random House LLC, 1745 Broadway, New York, NY 10019, and in Canada by Random House of Canada, a division of Penguin Random House Ltd., Toronto. Pictureback, Random House, and the Random House colophon are registered trademarks of Penguin Random House LLC. Nickelodeon, Dora and Friends, and all related titles, logos, and characters are trademarks of Viacom International Inc.
randomhousekids.com
ISBN 978-0-553-53836-6
Printed in the United States of America
10 9 8 7 6 5 4 3 2 1

One morning in Playa Verde, Dora and her friends were busy decorating for a special guest. Dora's friend Boots was coming all the way from the rainforest for a sleepover— and he was bringing Backpack and Map with him!

But when Boots arrived, he had some bad news. He had lost
Backpack and Map in the rainforest!
Dora hugged Boots. "It'll be okay, buddy. We'll find them!"

It was a long journey to the rainforest.

Dora and her friends traveled by bus . . .

by train . . .

and by boat. Finally, they arrived!

Boots led Dora and her friends to the riverbank.
"I put Backpack down here for a second, and—"
"Swiper took her," chimed a nearby voice. It
was the Chocolate Tree! He told Dora that Swiper
had gone to Blueberry Hill.

Just then, Dora and her friends saw Benny the Bull in his hot-air balloon!

"Cool ride, Benny!" said Pablo.

When Benny heard that Swiper had taken Backpack, he offered to give everyone a ride.

As they soared toward Blueberry Hill, Naiya spotted Swiper sneaking into Isa's garden!

The friends landed and found Isa with a small flower named Bud.

"Dora! I'm so excited to meet you. Are you going on an adventure?" he asked.

Dora nodded. "Come with us, Bud! *¡Vámonos!*"

The friends followed Swiper's tracks and found
the sneaky fox—but he didn't have Backpack or
Map. A big wind had blown them both away!

"Dora!" called a voice from above. It was Map.
He was whirling around in the wind!
Dora reached up . . . and caught Map!
Map told Dora that Backpack was stuck on
top of Tallest Mountain.

Everyone traveled together through the rainforest to Tallest Mountain.

"¡Mira!" shouted Dora. Backpack was dangling from a tree branch. But she wasn't alone. Tico was climbing up to try to save her!

A big gust of wind loosened some rocks.
They tumbled straight toward Tico!
"*¡Cuidado!*" called the friends.
"We've got to get Tico off the mountain!"
exclaimed Pablo.

Pablo and Benny guided the balloon toward the mountain. *"¡Salta, Tico!"* Kate cried as they got close to him.
Tico took an amazing jump—right into Kate's arms!
Tico was safe, but Backpack was still in trouble. Dora held up her magic charm bracelet. *"¡Cóndor mágico!"* she called.

A great condor appeared, and Dora hopped on—just as the branch holding Backpack broke! Swooping through the wild gusts of wind, Dora reached out and caught Backpack just in time! "*Mochila,* you're safe!" she cried.

Backpack was rescued, but the wind had torn a big hole in her.

"I can fix Backpack, but I'll need my sewing machine back in the city," declared Kate.

Dora and her friends jumped into Benny's balloon
and flew to Playa Verde.
Everyone waited anxiously as Kate went to work.

Finally, Kate emerged, proudly holding a patched Backpack decorated in amazing new colors. "She's all done!"

"Hey, Bud came back to Playa Verde, too!" Dora smiled at the little flower. "You can come with us on all our adventures!"

"*¡Todos juntos!*" everyone cheered.